Pebble™ Plus

Máquinas maravillosas/Mighty Machines

Ambulancias/Ambulances

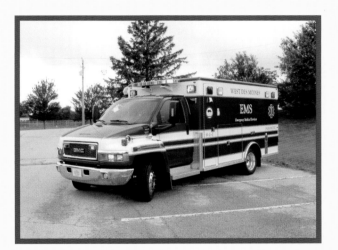

por/by Carol K. Lindeen

Traducción/Translation: Martín Luis Guzmán Ferrer, Ph.D.
Editor Consultor/Consulting Editor: Dra. Gail Saunders-Smith

Capstone press

Mankato, Minnesota

Pebble Plus is published by Capstone Press,
151 Good Counsel Drive, P.O. Box 669, Mankato, Minnesota 56002.
www.capstonepress.com

1 2 3 4 5 6 11 10 09 08 07 06

Library of Congress Cataloging-in-Publication Data
Lindeen, Carol K., 1976–
    [Ambulances. Spanish & English]
    Ambulancias/de Carol K. Lindeen=Ambulances/by Carol K. Lindeen.
    p. cm.—(Pebble plus: Máquinas maravillosas=Pebble plus. Mighty machines)
    Includes index.
    ISBN 13: 978-0-7368-5865-6 (hardcover)
    ISBN 10: 0-7368-5865-2 (hardcover)
    1. Ambulances—Juvenile literature. I. Title. II. Series Pebble plus. Máquinas maravillosas.
TL235.8.L56 2005
362.18'8—dc22   2005019047

Summary: Simple text and photographs present ambulances, their parts, and how emergency crews
use ambulances.

Editorial Credits
Martha E. H. Rustad, editor; Jenny Marks, bilingual editor; Eida del Risco, Spanish copy editor; Molly Nei,
    set designer; Kate Opseth and Ted Williams, book designers; Jo Miller, photo researcher; Scott Thoms,
    photo editor

Photo Credits
Capstone Press/Gary Sundermeyer, 19; Karon Dubke, cover
Corbis/Gabe Palmer, 6–7; Royalty-Free, 5
Daniel E. Hodges, 1, 9
Folio Inc./Novastock, 10–11
Getty Images Inc./The Image Bank/Pat LaCroix, 13
Index Stock Imagery/Mark Gibson, 20–21; Omni Photo Communications Inc., 14–15
911 Pictures, 17

**Pebble Plus thanks the Gold Cross Ambulance Service of Mankato, Minnesota, for its assistance
with photo shoots.**

Note to Parents and Teachers

The Mighty Machines set supports national standards related to science, technology, and
society. This book describes and illustrates ambulances. The images support early readers
in understanding the text. The repetition of words and phrases helps early readers learn
new words. This book also introduces early readers to subject-specific vocabulary words,
which are defined in the Glossary section. Early readers may need assistance to read
some words and to use the Table of Contents, Glossary, Internet Sites, and Index sections
of the book.

Table of Contents

Tabla de contenidos

What Are Ambulances?

Ambulances are vehicles
that take hurt or sick people
to hospitals.

¿Qué son las ambulancias?

Las ambulancias son vehículos
que llevan a personas
heridas o enfermas a
los hospitales.

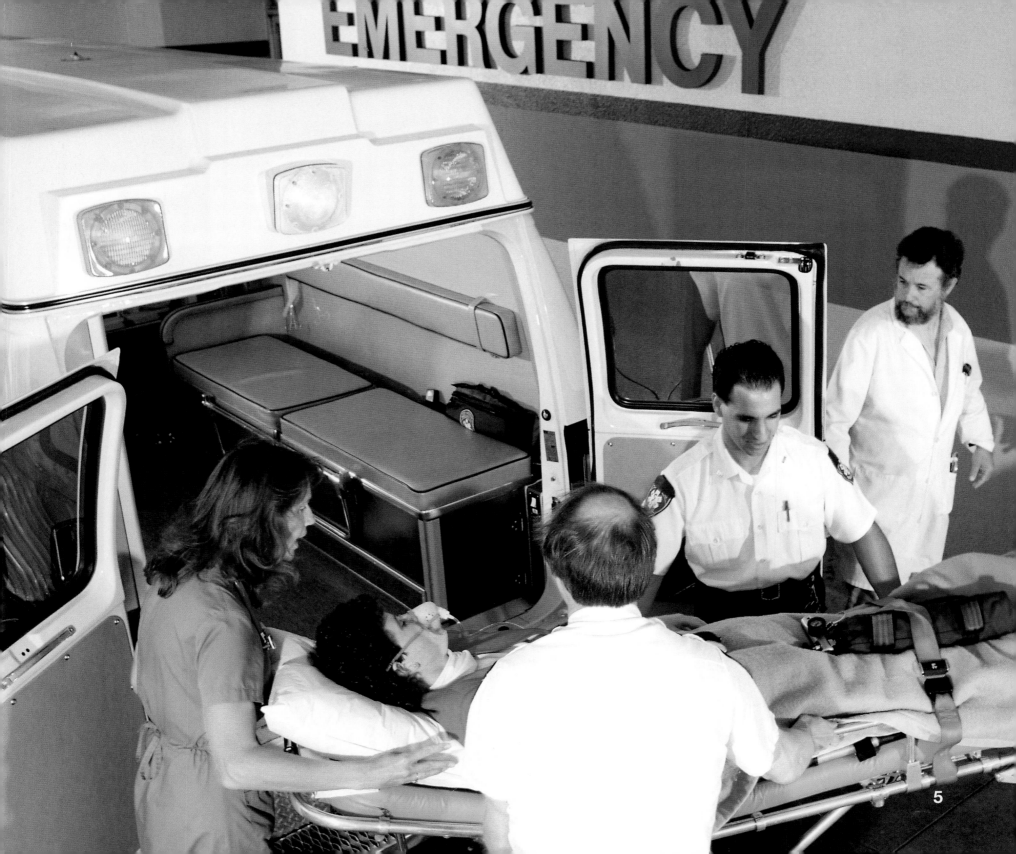

EMERGENCY

5

Ambulance Parts

Ambulances have
flashing lights and sirens.
They warn people that
an ambulance is coming.

Las partes de las ambulancias

Las ambulancias tienen sirenas
y luces centelleantes. Estas son
para avisar a la gente que va
a pasar una ambulancia.

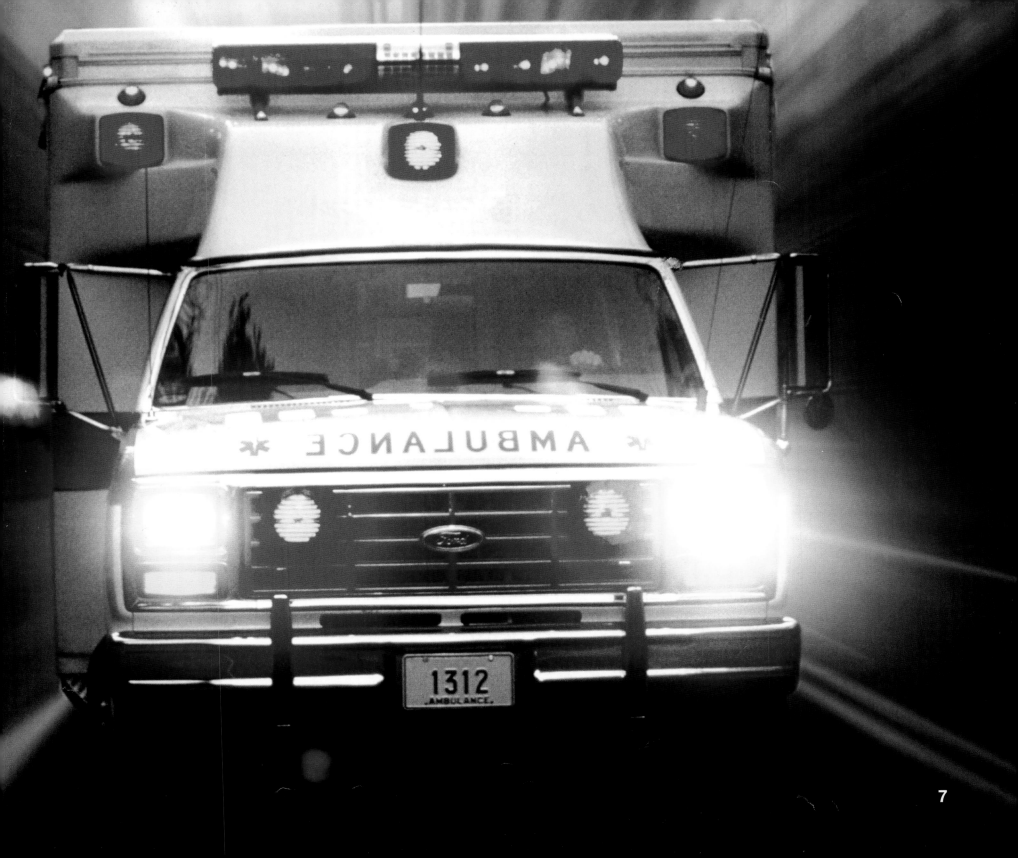

Ambulance drivers
sit in cabs. They talk
on the ambulance radio.
They turn on
the sirens and lights.

Los conductores de ambulancias
se sientan en una cabina.
Desde la ambulancia hablan
por un radio. Y encienden
las sirenas y las luces.

Hurt or sick people
ride in the back
of ambulances.
Supplies sit on shelves.

A los heridos o enfermos se
les lleva en la parte trasera de
la ambulancia. Los materiales
se ponen en anaqueles.

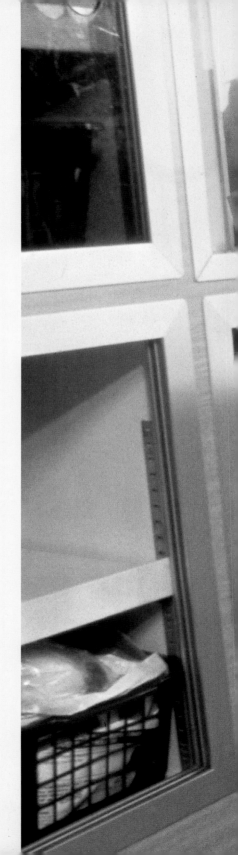

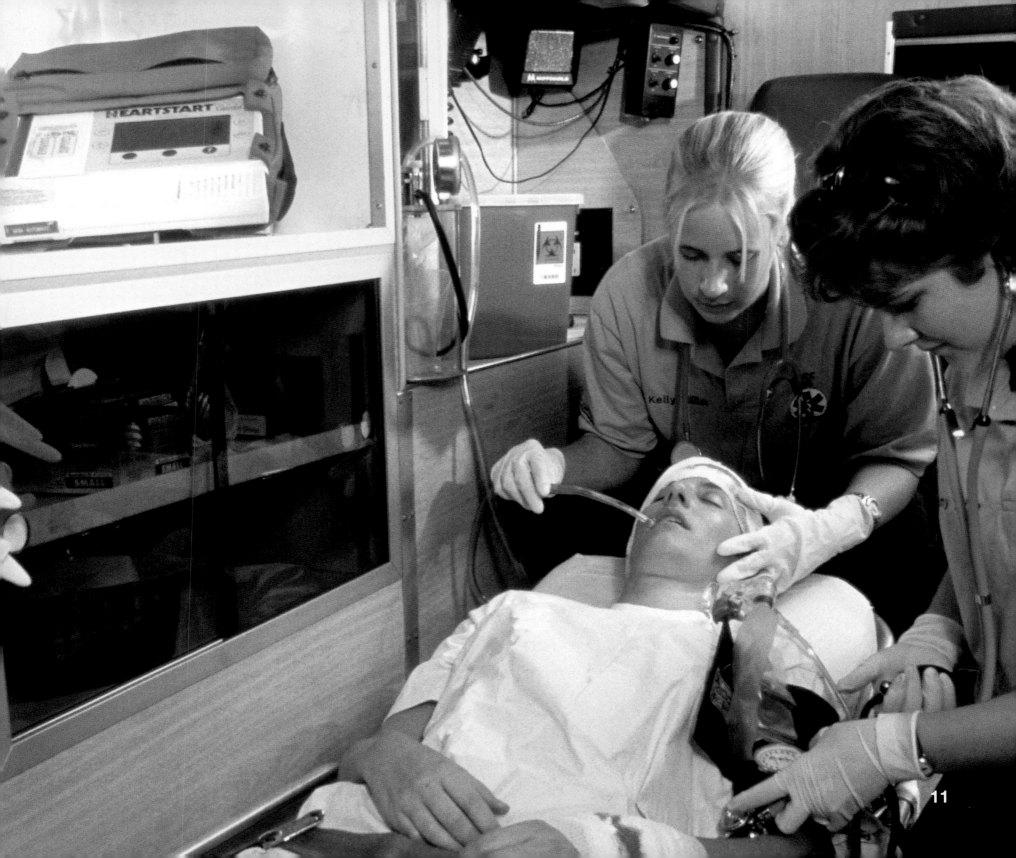

11

To the Rescue

An ambulance worker
gets a call on the radio.
Someone is hurt.

Auxilio

El trabajador de una ambulancia
recibe una llamada por el radio.
Alguien está herido.

The driver turns on
the sirens and lights.
The ambulance rushes
down the street.

El conductor enciende
las sirenas y las luces.
La ambulancia corre a toda
prisa por la calle.

The workers put the patient
on a stretcher.
They lift the stretcher
into the ambulance.

Los trabajadores ponen
al paciente en una camilla.
Levantan la camilla y
la meten en la ambulancia.

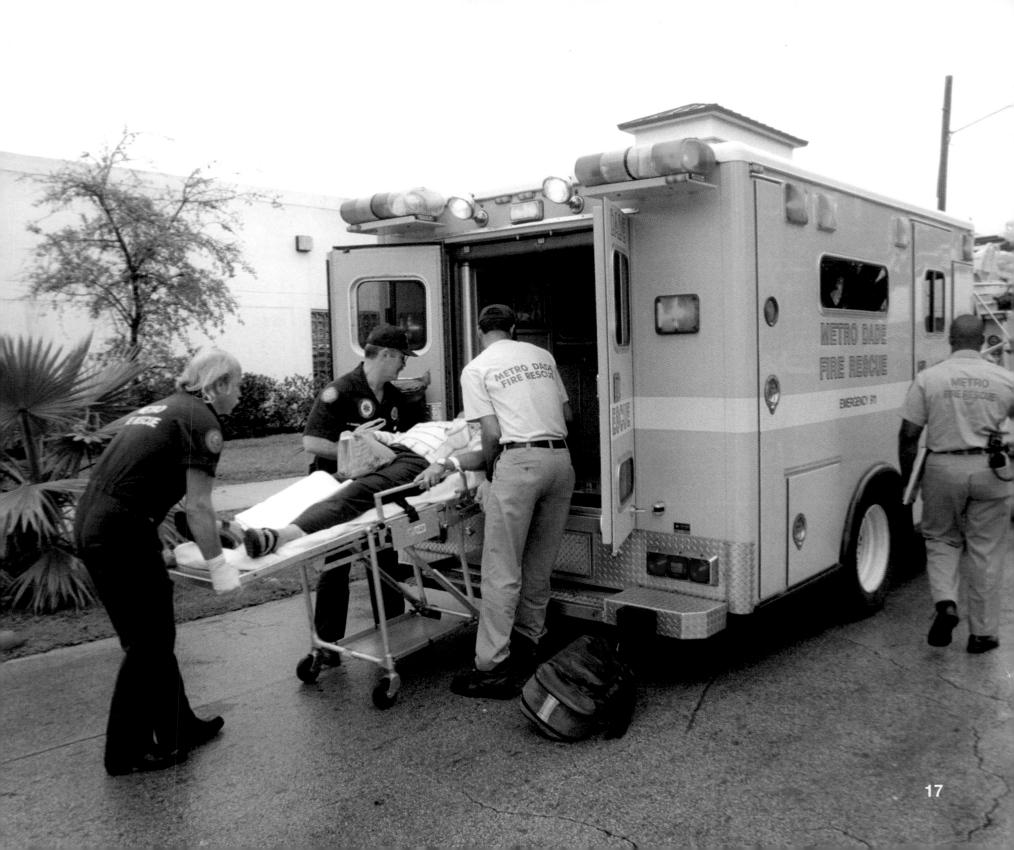

A worker takes care
of the patient.
The ambulance rushes
to the hospital.

Un trabajador cuida
al paciente.
La ambulancia corre
a toda prisa al hospital.

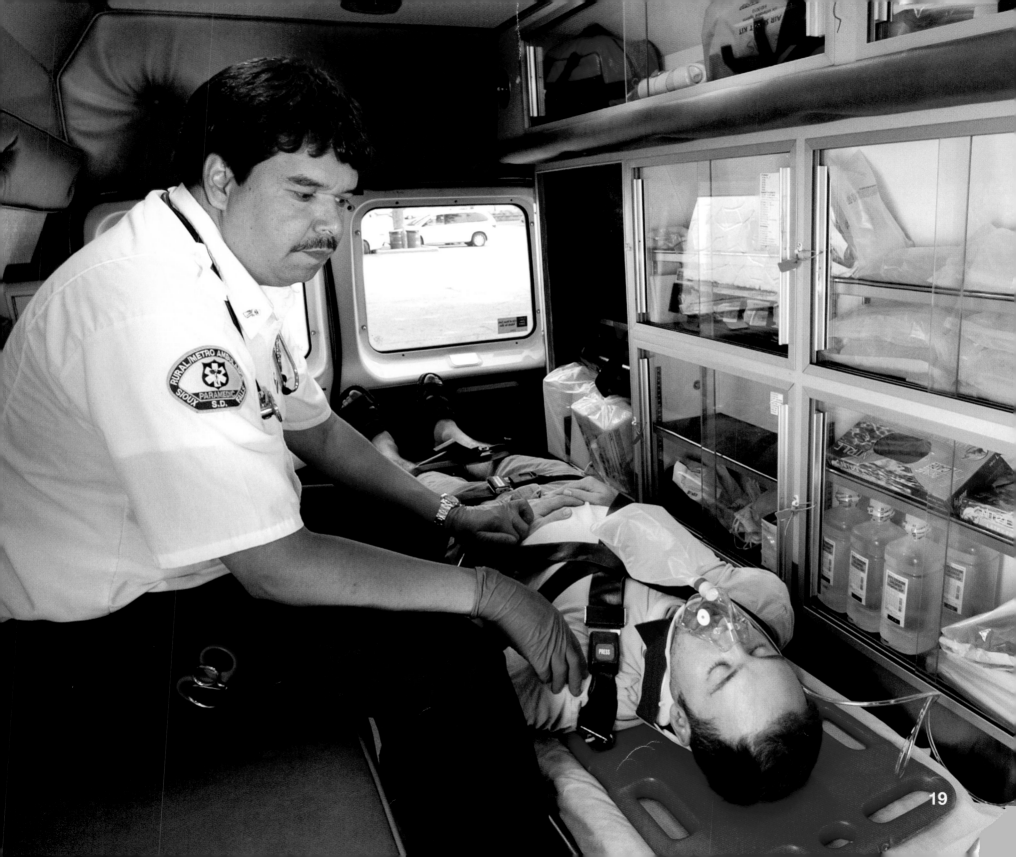

19

Workers use ambulances
to help people
in emergencies.

Los trabajadores usan
las ambulancias para ayudar
a la gente en emergencias.

Glossary

cab—the driver's area of a large truck or machine

emergency—something that happens with no warning and requires action right away

hospital—a place where doctors and nurses take care of sick or hurt people

patient—a person who is waiting for or getting medical care

siren—an object that makes a very loud sound as a warning

stretcher—a bed with wheels and legs that fold up; patients are strapped onto stretchers while in the ambulance.

vehicle—something that carries people or goods from one place to another; ambulances, police cars, and fire trucks are types of vehicles.

Glosario

cabina—lugar donde se sienta el conductor en un camión grande o en una máquina

camilla—una camita con ruedas y patas que se doblan; los pacientes se sujetan con tiras a la camilla mientras están en la ambulancia.

emergencia—algo que sucede sin aviso y que hay que atender enseguida

hospital—lugar donde los médicos y las enfermeras cuidan a los enfermos o heridos

paciente—persona que espera o recibe atención médica

sirena—objeto que hace un ruido muy alto como señal de peligro

vehículo—máquina que lleva a personas y artículos de un lugar a otro; las ambulancias, las patrullas de policía y los camiones de bomberos son diferentes tipos de vehículos.

Internet Sites

FactHound offers a safe, fun way to find Internet sites related to this book. All of the sites on FactHound have been researched by our staff.

Here's how:

1) Visit *www.facthound.com*

2) Type in this special code **0736836527** for age-appropriate sites. Or enter a search word related to this book for a more general search.

3) Click on the **FETCH IT** button.

FactHound will fetch the best sites for you!

Sitios de Internet

FactHound te ofrece una manera segura y divertida para encontrar sitios de Internet relacionados con este libro. Todos los sitios de FactHound han sido investigados por nuestro equipo. Es posible que los sitios no estén en español.

Así:

1) Ve a *www.facthound.com*

2) Teclea la clave especial **0736836527** para los sitios apropiados por edad. O teclea una palabra relacionada con este libro para una búsqueda más general.

3) Clic en el botón de **FETCH IT**.

¡FactHound buscará los mejores sitios para ti!